FUNNY POEMS

Illustrated by Stephen Cartwright

Selected by Heather Amery

Poems by

Dave Calder, Elizabeth Chorley, Pie Corbett,
John Cotton, Peter Dixon, John Foster, Trevor Harvey, Michael Johnson,
Kevin McCann, Shelagh McGee, Robin Mellor, Trevor Millum, Brian Moses,
Irene Rawnsley, Vernon Scannell, Matt Simpson, Matthew Sweeney.

With thanks to Lois Beeson

Up and Away

Little Daisy Dittersdorf
    Decided she would fly:
"I'll make some wings and flap them
    And tootle round the sky!"

She fetched some bits of bamboo
    To make herself a frame
Which she covered up with silver foil
    Then painted on her name.

She strapped the wings upon her back
    And balanced on the fence.
She said "I'm going to go to Zanzibar!"
    We haven't seen her since.

Matt Simpson

Turning Points

Yesterday
Our teacher
Told us the story   "That's nothing!"
Of Lot's wife   Said Tracey Saunders.
Who looked back   "My mum was backing the car
And was turned   And when she looked round
Into a pillar of salt.   She'd turned into a ditch!"

John Foster

Enquire Within

"Is there anybody there?" asked the pupil,
Knocking on the staffroom door.
"You'll be lucky!" the cleaner answered,
"It's almost ten minutes past four!'

Trevor Harvey

My Sister's Knitting

My sister's sitting knitting
Each day she'll sit and knit,
Clicking garments into shape,
Wondering who they'll fit.
Long johns for Uncle Arthur,
Who tends to feel the cold,
(It's one of the discomforts
Of being rather old).
Short socks for Cousin Doris,
Who does a lot of walking;
A muffler for Gladys
Who does a lot of talking.
For Grandmama a bonnet,
(Two plain, three purl, slip one),
And this round thing's a cushion
For the cat to sit upon.
My sister's sitting knitting,
and I am all agog
To see my sister fitting
Woolly bloomers on the dog!

Shelagh McGee

3

Leonora

Leonora the Terrible
gritted her teeth
and, as she ran,
crushed three boys beneath
her pounding feet.
She crossed the yard
with seven league steps
and ignited the staffroom
with her fiery breath.
Her attention then turned
to the teachers who
were running about
not knowing what to do.
She opened her mouth
and with a dreadful roar
said, *I won't come to
your school, any more!*

Robin Mellor

Old Mother Hubbard

Old Mother Hubbard
Sat in the cupboard
Eating Jack's Christmas pie;
He opened the door
Gave a furious roar
And blacked Mother Hubbard's right eye.

Vernon Scannell

Sunday in the Yarm Fard

The mat keowed
The mow cooed
The bog darked
The kigeon pooed

The squicken chalked
The surds bang
The kwuk dacked
The burch rells chang

And then, after all the dacking and the changing,
The chalking and the banging,
The darking and the pooing,
The keowing and the cooing . . .
There was a mewtiful beaumont
Of queace and pie-ate.

Trevor Millum

The Young Lady of Lynn

There was a young lady of Lynn,
Who was so uncommonly thin
That when she essayed
To drink lemonade,
She slipped through the straw and fell in.

Anon

Elephantastic

Six great grey elephants
were taking tea with me:
Mmmm, jungle sandwiches and savannah scones.
    Brr Brr Brr Brr
The quiet one went to take a trunk-call telephone.

Five great grey elephants
were taking tea with me.
A mammoth munching, scrunching session;
    Chomp Chomp Chomp
Then the loud one left for special trumpet lessons.

Four great grey elephants
were taking tea with me:
sticky stalks, fruit bursting at the seams.
    Squeaking speaking!
The small one heard a mouse. He ran away to scream . . .

Three great grey elephants
were taking tea with me.
Finished, bulging fat, sitting back, relaxed.
    Smash Splinter Crash
The big one's garden chair suddenly collapsed.

Two great grey elephants
were taking tea with me:
seven heaven-empty plates, seven heaven-empty cups.
    Splish Splash Splosh
Gigantic had a nosey-hose way of washing up.

One great grey elephant
is drying plates and cups and cutlery.
An extra-extraordinary sight for me to see?
    No No No No
No, because I'm a great grey elephant. Yes, me.
    Perhaps Maybe
Or was it just my tea-time elephantasy?

Michael Johnson

Little Bo Peep

Little Bo Peep has lost her sheep,
Her marbles, too – it could make you weep –
Dozy Boy Blue has gone to sleep;
Jack and Jill can't stay on their feet.

Spratt and his wife have nothing to eat.
Miss Muffet's scared of a harmless spider,
Contrary Mary? Who could abide her?
The Piper's son is a common thief
Who fully deserves to come to grief.

I bet Tommy Tucker's voice was a pain –
As bad as that kid's who howled in the lane.
So why pick on Simon? Simple? He
Doesn't seem as daft as the others to me!

Vernon Scannell

7

Big-head Dragon

O there once was a dragon
Who was given to braggin',
Who would bawl and would yell
                 At
                      the top of
                            his
                              voice:

"I'm a rather swish dragon
With my spikey tail waggin';
Assume from the flames
                 That
                   my breath's
                      very
                         choice!

I munch lots of maidens
That I snatch on my raidin's;
I gobble them down
                 With
                   my
                     bulldozer
                        jaws!

I'm a gorgeous green monster,
I'm a son-of-a-gun, sir,
With teeth yucky-yellow
                 But
                   as fierce
                     as
                     sharp saws.

Should any daft knight, sir,
Step into my sight, sir,
I'll freeze his blood cold
                 With my
                   lasering red
                      eyes!

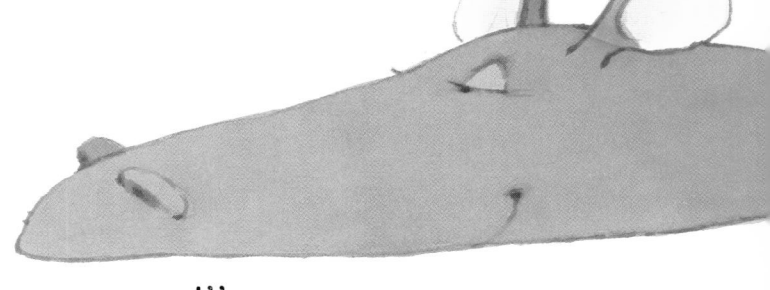

I'm a smasher, I'm terrific,
I'm as great as the Pacific,
Chomping off the heads
        Of those tin can guys!''

Matt Simpson

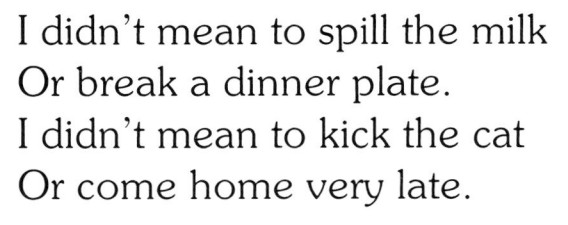

I Didn't Mean To

I didn't mean to spill the milk
Or break a dinner plate.
I didn't mean to kick the cat
Or come home very late.

I didn't mean to tear my dress
Or lose the front door key
I didn't mean to lie a bit.
You're always blaming me.

I didn't mean to frighten Gran
Or pull away her chair.
I didn't mean to burn the toast,
Get butter in my hair.

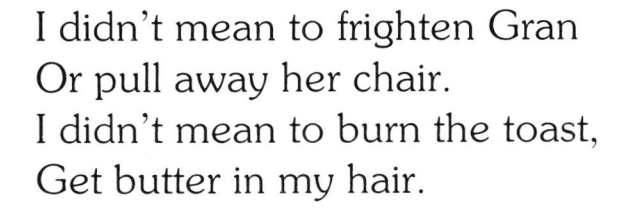

I didn't mean to make Mum cross
Or eat up all the cakes.
I didn't mean to make excuses
But everyone makes mistakes.

Elizabeth Chorley

The Flying Spring Onion

The flying spring onion
   flew through the air
     over to where
the tomatoes grew in rows
   and he said to those
     seed-filled creatures
My rooted days are done,
   so while you sit here
     sucking sun
I'll be away and gone,
   to Greenland
     where they eat no green
     and I won't be seen
in a salad bowl with you,
   stung by lemon,
     greased by oil,
and nothing at all to do
   except wait to be eaten.
With that he twirled
   his green propellors
and rose above the rows
   of red balls
who stared as he grew small
   and disappeared.

          Matthew Sweeney

I Had a Little Brother

I had a little brother
His name was Tiny Tim,
I put him in a bath tub
To teach him how to swim.

He drank up all the water,
He ate up all the soap,
He died last night
With a bubble in his throat.

In came the doctor,
In came the nurse,
In came the lady
With the alligator purse.

"Dead", said the doctor,
"Dead", said the nurse,
"Dead", said the lady
With the alligator purse.

Out went the doctor,
Out went the nurse,
Out went the lady
With the alligator purse.

          Anon

Problems with the Moon

When the moon fell into our garden
it took an awful lot of my
pushing and shoving
and swearing from Dad
to get it back up in the sky.

First we all leaned shoulders to it
and pushed when Dad called "Heave her";
it wouldn't move and Mum stepped back
suggesting we use a big lever.

So Dad got a plank from the garage
and I got one from the shed;
we tried them both, and the moonbeams rolled
right over Mum's best flower bed.

"Oh drat!" said Mum in anger,
"The blessed thing!" said Dad,
the moon slipped on to his greenhouse
and the things he said then were pretty bad.

Eventually our efforts succeeded
and, as Dad gave a mighty roar,
the moon shot up and outwards
and lodged in the sky once more.

Yes – when the moon fell into our garden
it took an awful lot of my
pushing and shoving
and swearing from Dad
to get it back up in the sky.

Robin Mellor

11

I Was Just . . .

I was just
Teaching our cat to swim
And suddenly
The bathroom was flooded.

I was just
Looking at Dad's razor
And suddenly
Our cat had a bald patch.

I was just
Seeing if our cat could fly
And suddenly
There's a hole in the shed roof.

I was just
Wondering if our cat had nine lives:
It didn't.

I was just wondering
What's the worst feeling in the world?
And now I really know.

Kevin McCann

Doing Topics

At School we do Topics.
I always do "Birds".
I quite like the drawings
but can't do the words.

Pie Corbett

Tall Story

He lives in the chimney
since he grew so tall
he couldn't fit
inside the house at all;

Dad takes a ladder
round to the back;
feeds my brother
at the chimney stack.

He likes an umbrella
when a wet wind blows
and woolly socks
to warm his toes

and we take it in turns
when the weather's fine
to sit on the roof
and talk to him.

But we don't like
the comments people make;
you'd think sometimes
it was our mistake

having a tall person
in the family;
my brother's
an ordinary you or me;

So we're going to move,
where living's cheaper;
Dad's got a job
as a lighthouse keeper.

Irene Rawnsley

13

ORChestra

What's that sound undelightful –
A noise fiendish and frightful –
Like the wailing of ghouls at the moon?
As the gruesome sound grows,
You wince, curl your toes . . .
It's the orc orchestra rehearsing its tunes!

The string section stands:
A bristling band
Of warriors of the night;
Their violins raised,
Their bug-eyes glazed
With musical delight.

A fearsome troll
Gives a fine drum roll
And a gremlin plays the tuba;
The orc octet
Play their clarinets
Like they were sticks of rhubarb.

There's a group of elves
Who hold themselves
With grandeur and with grace . . .
They play trombones
And finger-bones
At a fine foot-tapping pace.

There's a minotaur,
Who straddles the floor
And snorts through his great bull-nose;
And he grasps the bass
Like a battle mace
Smack-thwacking through his foes.

The woodwinds soar,
The flugelhorns roar
And the conductor swirls his stick,
While the dwarves play flutes
And lilting lutes
Allegro – or pretty quick!

Oh, now, don't be dismayed
At the way they play;
They really aren't going to bite you!
They may seem ferocious
And their music atrocious
But – they're doing their best to delight you!   *Trevor Millum*

The Young Lady of Riga

There was a young lady of Riga,
Who rode with a smile on a tiger;
They returned from the ride
With the lady inside,
And the smile on the face of the tiger.   *Anon*

I Don't Want To Shrink

I don't want to get smaller,
I don't want to shrink,
if I wash too much I'll be
washed down the sink.
Mum keeps on saying
"Go and have a good wash."
but if I'm clean all the time
I'll look shiny and posh.
Have you seen what happens
to soap in the bath?
it gets smaller and smaller,
no . . . don't laugh,
it isn't funny to be washed away,
to get withered and wrinkled,

to disappear down the sink.
I don't want to get smaller,
dirt does me no harm,
I don't want to shrink. Anyway,
dirt keeps me warm.

Robin Mellor

Into the Mixer

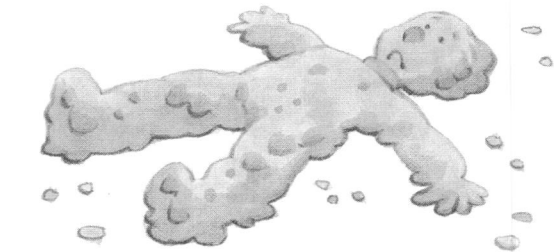

Into the mixer he went,
　　the nosy boy,
into the mess of wet cement,
　　round and round
　　with a glugging sound
and a boyish screamed complaint.

Out of the mixer he came,
　　the concrete boy,
on to the road made of the same
　　quick-setting stuff.
　　He looked rough
and he'd only himself to blame.

Matthew Sweeney

Call in the Vet

Sir Silas Debret
had to call in the vet
When the pigs in the sty
Turned blue.

"Dear Doctor," he sighed,
"I think someone's dyed
My especially imported
Pig stew!"

The vet took his soap,
A large stethoscope
And went in the sty
For a look.

Yes, the pigs were quite blue
And just what to do
Didn't appear
in his Book.

He thought and he thought
More than he ought,
Until he came up with
The answer.

"If I may be so bold,
These pigs are too cold!
What they need is some
Warm woolly pants, sir!"

Sir Silas Debret,
Without a regret,
Set all his farmhands
A-knitting,

Till after two Sundays
The pigs' thermal undies
Were finally ready
For fitting.

Even though it was snowing,
Soon the pigs were all glowing
And the snowflakes
Just melted away.

They all looked so pink
You couldn't help think
Of cherry trees
Blossoming in May.

"By George, Dr Figgs,
I've not seen my pigs
Ever before look
So frisky!"

Beamed Sir Silas Debret
Shaking hands with the vet
And pouring him out
Some malt whisky.

Matt Simpson

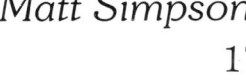

An Unspelling Bea

An unspelling bea, an unspelling bea
i buzz abart for ours u sea
Amungst blewbells and croakuss
And other flours, not making a fuss
As i serch for hunny and land on pedals
Making shore that nobody medals
With this sharp stinging
Humming-singing
Unspelling bea
Who seems to have lost his dictionree!

John Cotton

Pardon!

My mother stared,
My father glared,
I hung my head in shame.
But in the next long quiet bit,
I burped
and burped again.

Elizabeth Chorley

An Atrocious Pun

A major, with wonderful force,
Called out in Hyde Park for a horse.
All the flowers looked round,
But no horse could be found,
So he just rhododendron, of course.

Anon

18

Our Teacher

Our teacher taps his toes,
keeping the beat to some silent tune,
only he knows.

Our teacher drums his fingers,
on his desk, on the window,
on anything, when the room is quiet,
when we're meant to be writing,
in silence.

Our teacher cracks his knuckles,
clicks his fingers, grinds his teeth,
his knees are knocking the edge of his desk,
he breathes to a rhythmical beat.

When he turns his head in a certain way,
there's a bone that cracks in his neck.
When he sinks to the floor,
we often think, he'll stay on his knees
forever more, he's such a physical wreck!

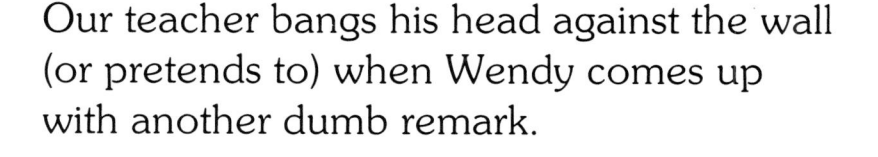

Our teacher bangs his head against the wall
(or pretends to) when Wendy comes up
with another dumb remark.

Our teacher says we annoy him
with all our silly fuss.
Perhaps he's never really thought
how much he irritates us.

Brian Moses

Stop Me If You've Heard It Already

Once upon a time
in a kingdom far away
there lived an old old woman
in a gingerbread café.
She had three strapping sons
two ugly daughters who told lies
and a beautiful sad stepdaughter
who was a giant in disguise.
Now one day a knight passed by
running off to sea with a kipper
and dropped a golden frog
that laid a talking slipper
which the youngest son then sold
for a magic mashed potato
that ate his elder brothers
and began to grow and grow.
It put the young boy on its back
and flew off across the fields;
his sisters pedalled after it
on their spinning wheels.
They crossed a soggy river
they climbed a glass beanstalk
they caught that bad potato
with a knife and fork.
It turned into a princess,

and such was their surprise
the beautiful sad stepdaughter
grew forty-nine feet high
and the other sisters, curtseying,
(for they were awful snobs)
were squashed beneath her giant feet
into two shapeless blobs.
And when the old old woman
saw this on her TV
she sent a storm that drowned the
knight
that very night at sea.
The storm came roaring back again
and with a mighty clout
it knocked the old old woman
upside down and inside out.
It wrapped the giant in a cloud
and drowned it in despair
which made the son dissolve in tears
and vanish in thin air.
The poor potato-faced princess
was crushed by this disaster
and then there was nobody left at all
to live happily *ever* after.

Dave Calder

The Painting Lesson

"What's THAT dear?"
asked the new teacher.

"It's Mummy," I replied.

"But Mums aren't green and orange!
You really haven't TRIED.
You don't just paint in SPLODGES
– You're old enough to know
You need to THINK before you work . . .
Now – have another go."

She helped me draw two arms and legs,
A face with sickly smile,
A rounded body, dark brown hair,
A hat – and, in a while,
She stood back (with her face bright pink):
"That's SO much better – don't you think?"

But she turned white
At ten to three
When an orange-green blob
Collected me.

"Hi, mum!"

Trevor Harvey

21

Conversation with an Alien

Well, I was sitting in the garden,
the day was nearly done,
and I lounged about on the patio
in the rays of the setting sun,
when up above, and to the right,
I heard a wheezing sigh,
like that the baby tends to make
when he is going to cry.

So I looked up and there I saw,
dropping down from the sky,
a sort of blue teapot without a lid
and I wondered that it could fly.
It landed right in front of me,
in the middle of the garden,
a door slid open and out he came,
a *Thingy*, if the expression you'll pardon.

With curiosity I looked at him
and from my seat I rose,
walked over, smiled, and nervously said,
"You're invading us, I suppose?"
He looked at me, looking at him,
I looked at him as he looked at me,
he was green (of course) and spiky too
with three legs and yellow knees.

"What is your name?" I said to him,
he answered not a word.
The Alien and I stood silently,

it was really quite absurd.
So slowly I repeated my words
and asked the question again,
"You're from outer space, I can see", I said,
"Please, will you tell me your name?"

And he said, "Bleebleoople."
and I said "Pardon?"
And he said "Bleebleoople."
and I said "What?"
And he said "Bleebleoople."
and I said "Oh."

"So where are you from?" I asked
And he said "Trimpleslicksness"
and I said "Pardon?"
And he said "Trimpleslicksness"
and I said "What?"
And he said "Trimpleslicksness"
and I said "Oh."

"So, what have you come for?" I asked.
"Trippledizzies, slippleoodle", he said
and I said "Pardon?"
"Trippledizzies, slippleoodle", he said
and I said "What?"
"Trippledizzies, slippleoodle", he said
and I said "Oh."

He turned back to his space ship,
"Where are you going?" I cried,
And he said "Ziproodlooses"
and I said "Pardon?"
And he said "Ziproodlooses"
and I said "What?"
And he said *"You Humans never listen!"*
and I said "Oh . . .
. . . goodbye."

Robin Mellor

To the Moon

O Moon! when I look on your beautiful face
Careering along through the darkness of space,
The thought has quite frequently come to my mind
If ever I'll gaze on your lovely behind.

Anon

Big Boots

Suppose I wore
size ninety-nine boots,
I'd walk in mud
wherever I found it.

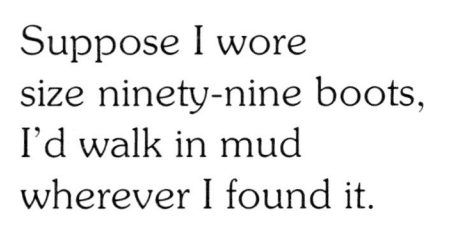

I'd make
a trail of footprints
down the street
so that people
would say,
Let's hurry away;
a giant
or a monster
or a yeti
or a dinosaur
or a great big
hairy gorilla
came this way!

I'd keep my boots
in the garden shed,
and hang my big feet
out of bed.

Irene Rawnsley

The Strawberry Cried

The strawberry cried
"I'm in a jam!
I don't know why
But here I am."

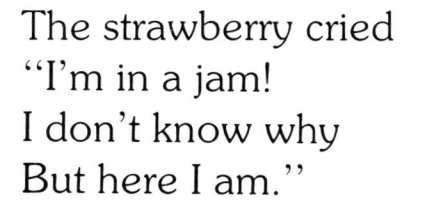

The little tart
Said, "So I see.
I know because
the jam's in me."

And Tubby Tibbs,
The greedy lad,
Devouring both
Said, "Just too bad!"

Vernon Scannell

The Man of Bengal

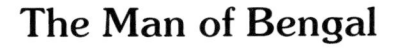

There once was a man of Bengal
Who was asked to a fancy dress ball;
He murmured: "I'll risk it
and go as a biscuit . . ."
But a dog ate him up in the hall.

Anon

Please Sir!!

There's a fight – Sir!!
In the cloakrooms . . . Sir!!
And Arnie's strangled Paul.
Smithy's strangled Watson
'cos Watson took his ball.
Barney's ripped his shirt . . . Sir,
And Baker sput on Sue.
She was only tryin' to stop them
And she's got it on her shoe . . .
The helper lady went . . . Sir,
She said she couldn't stay.
Jane's crying in the toilets
And the gerbil's got away . . . .

Garnett knocked the cage . . . Sir,
The door, it just flipped back,
And it ran behind the cupboard
And it's stuck inside a crack.
We poked it with a stick . . . Sir,
But the powder paint got spilt.
It's over all the carpet
And it's over Helen's kilt.
I think you ought to come . . . Sir,
Mildred Miles was sick
And all the boys are yellin'
And Martin threw a brick.
It nearly hit John Baily.
And he's goin' to tell his Mum,
So shall I say you're comin'
and shall I fetch his Mum?

Shall we get the cleaners?
And can I mop the paint?
The new boy's torn his jacket
And he thinks he's going to faint . . .
The other teachers said . . . Sir,
That I should come to you
'Cos you're the Duty Teacher
So you'll know what to do
Sir.

Peter Dixon

Fathers' Race

Tony's dad goes jogging,
Gareth's dad lifts weights.
Leroy's dad's a stunt man,
Errol's dad jumps gates!

Trixie's dad plays football
for a fourth division team.
Rachel's dad's a sprinter,
fast and flash and lean.

Simon Miller's dad
enters marathons.
I've seen him training hard,
running from Simon's mum!

But my dad's thin and weedy
he's bound to lose the race.
He'll stumble and trip or worse,
fall flat upon his face.

I know my friends will laugh
and call me awful names.
Please don't enter the race, dad,
it's me who gets the blame!

Brian Moses

The Old Lady of Rye

There was an old lady of Rye
Who was baked by mistake in a pie,
To the household's disgust
She emerged through the crust,
And exclaimed, with a yawn, 'Where am I?'

Anon

The Sleuth

I longed to be a Private Eye
But there were hordes of those;
So I filled a gap in sleuthing work
And became – a Private Nose.

I sniffed out clues as best I could,
But didn't do too well;
It was because I'd overlooked
I lacked a sense of smell.

"You're just a Drip!" my clients cried.
"Why did we pick a Nose?"
I thus gave up on nostril work
And became – a Set of Toes.

I crept about to stalk my prey
Who didn't give "two hoots";
They knew EXACTLY where I was –
I'd put on squeaky boots.

From Private Nose to Private Toes,
My life has been a failure!
I wonder if they're short of Eyes
In Hong Kong – or Australia?

Trevor Harvey

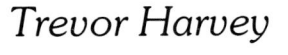

Peasy!

You want me to do that ten figure sum,
          that's peasy!
Wind my legs over that bar,
slide down into a forward roll
with a double back flip to follow,
          that's peasy!
Build a working model of Big Ben
from Technical Lego,
Huh, peasy!
Clear that five foot hurdle in one leap,
cross country run up a mountain peak,
keep writing a story for one whole week,
          peasy!
Score thirty goals in record time,
in ten minutes write a thousand lines,
say 'Supercalifragilisticexpialidocious' two hundred
times, backwards,
          Oh that's peasy!
BUT . . .
eat the skin off of custard.
Ugh! That's the toughest thing in the world!

Brian Moses

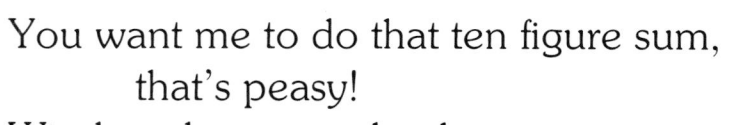

Did You Ever Go Fishing?

Did you ever go fishing on a bright, sunny day?
Sit on a fence and have the fence give way?
Slide off the fence and rip your pants,
And see the little fishes do the hootchy-kootchy dance?   *Anon*

28

The Great Computer

Professor Ditherspoon-Wombat,
Working all alone,
Built the greatest computer
The world had ever known.

He made micro-chips from potatoes
And his dolly mixture transistors
Were all linked up with chewing gum
And hair grips of his sister's;

Got a mega-byte from a dinosaur,
From a bi-plane unbolted a joystick,
Made floppy discs from a halibut
And a keyboard out of Blu Tack.

And when he had constructed it
Quite to his satisfaction
He decided he would type in
Some very knotty questions.

For example: how many beans make five?
How does your garden grow?
How much is that dog in the window?
Where do flies in winter go?

The answer to the first one
Came out as "93",
To the second: "Oh, the usual!"
To the third: "As much as me!"

But when it tried to work out
The answer to Question Four
Its fuses flew like fireworks
And it melted all over the floor.

Matt Simpson

Ambrose Visits His Aunt

When Ambrose went to visit his aunty
it was for the very first time;
he wanted to make a good impression,
wanted the afternoon to be fine.

But he tripped when he stood on the doorstep
and banged his head on the door,
so when his aunty opened it up
he was lying on the floor.

She took him into the kitchen
to have a cup of tea,
he sat on the cat (asleep on the chair)
and caught the table with his knee.

This jogged the cups and saucers
and spilt the milk on the cloth,
the teapot teetered on the edge
and, with a crash, it fell right off.

Ambrose bent to pick up the pieces
and slipped on the tea stained floor,
flattened the jugs on the dresser
and put his foot through the door.

At this point in the proceedings
his uncle came into the room
and looked at the chaos around him
with a face that looked like Doom.

Ambrose said that he would help them
to clear the mess he had made,
but they tied him to an armchair
and gave him some lemonade.

No further catastrophe happened,
for they wouldn't let Ambrose move,
and when he said "Thanks for having me",
his aunt said something rude.

Ambrose waved goodbye to his aunty
and started on his way home;
he walked carefully down the narrow path
and fell over a garden gnome.

Robin Mellor

Not a Word
They walked the lane together,
The sky was dotted with stars.
They reached the rails together,
He lifted up the bars.
She neither smiled nor thanked him,
Because she knew not how,
For he was only the farmer's boy
And she was the jersey cow!

Anon

Index of first lines

The publishers wish to thank the following for permission to reproduce the poems in this book:
Dave Calder for "Stop Me If You've Heard It Already"; Elizabeth Chorley for "I Didn't Mean To", "Pardon"; Pie Corbett for "Doing Topics"; John Cotton for "An Unspelling Bea"; Peter Dixon for "Please Sir!!", John Foster for "Turning Points"; Trevor Harvey for "Enquire Within", "The Painting Lesson", "The Sleuth"; Michael Johnson for "Elephantastic"; Kevin McCann for "I Was Just . . ."; Shelagh McGee for "My Sister's Knitting"; Robin Mellor for "Ambrose Visits His Aunt", "Conversation with an Alien", "I Don't Want to Shrink", "Leonora", "Problems with the Moon"; Trevor Millum for "ORChestra", "Sunday in the Yarm Fard"; Brian Moses for "Fathers' Race", "Our Teacher", "Peasy!"; Irene Rawnsley for "Big Boots", "Tall Story"; Vernon Scannell for "Little Bo Peep", "Old Mother Hubbard", "The Strawberry Cried"; Matt Simpson for "Big-head Dragon", "Call in the Vet", "The Great Computer", "Up and Away"; Matthew Sweeney for "Into The Mixer", "The Flying Spring Onion".

The publishers have made every effort to trace copyright holders and would be grateful to hear from any not here acknowledged.

First published in 1990. Usborne Publishing Limited, Usborne House, 83-85 Saffron Hill, London EC1N 8RT, England. This collection © Usborne Publishing Ltd. 1990. The individual copyrights belong to the authors. The illustrations © Usborne Publishing Ltd. 1990. The name Usborne and the device 🐝 are Trade Marks of Usborne Publishing Limited. All rights reserved. No part of this publication may be stored in a retrieval system or transmitted in any form or by any means, electronic, mechanical, photocopy, recording or otherwise, without the prior permission of the publisher.

Printed in Belgium.
Universal Edition

For Annabelle
— BC

For Lucille Johnson-Walker, a businesswoman, the counselor
and grandmother of our neighborhood. Your voice has been
amplified throughout this book. Stand UP and Stand OUT!
We hear you.
— CAJ

Text copyright © 2022 by Brittney Cooper
Illustrations copyright © 2022 by Cathy Ann Johnson

All rights reserved. Published by Orchard Books, an imprint of Scholastic Inc., *Publishers since 1920.* ORCHARD BOOKS and
design are registered trademarks of Watts Publishing Group, Ltd., used under license. SCHOLASTIC and associated logos
are trademarks and/or registered trademarks of Scholastic Inc. • The publisher does not have any control over and
does not assume any responsibility for author or third-party websites or their content. • No part of this publication
may be reproduced, stored in a retrieval system, or transmitted in any form or by any means, electronic, mechanical,
photocopying, recording, or otherwise, without written permission of the publisher. For information regarding permission,
write to Scholastic Inc., Attention: Permissions Department, 557 Broadway, New York, NY 10012.

Library of Congress Cataloging-in-Publication Data
Names: Cooper, Brittney C., 1980– author. | Johnson, Cathy Ann, 1964– illustrator. • Title: Stand up! : ten mighty women
who made a change / Brittney Cooper, Cathy Ann Johnson. • Description: New York : Scholastic Inc., [2022] | Audience:
Ages 4–8 | Audience: Grades PreK–3 | Summary: "Biographical collection of ten female figures who changed the
world by standing up for what's right and offering an inspirational call to action, reminding everyone that they can
be forces for change when they stand up!"—Provided by publisher. • Identifiers: LCCN 2021040595 (print) | LCCN
2021040596 (ebook) | ISBN 9781338763850 (hardcover) | ISBN 9781338815450 (ebk) • Subjects: LCSH: African
American women political activists—Biography—Juvenile literature. | Black women—Biography—Juvenile literature.
| Political participation—Juvenile literature. | Social action—Juvenile literature. | Assertiveness in children—Juvenile
literature. | BISAC: JUVENILE FICTION / People & Places / United States / African American & Black | JUVENILE
NONFICTION / Social Topics / Prejudice & Racism • Classification: LCC E185.6.C773 2022 (print) | LCC E185.6
(ebook) | DDC 920.72/08996073—dc23 • LC record available at https://lccn.loc.gov/2021040595 • LC ebook
record available at https://lccn.loc.gov/2021040596
10 9 8 7 6 5 4 3 2 1   22 23 24 25 26
Printed in China   62 • First edition, August 2022
Book design by Doan Buu
The text type was set in Twentieth Century. The display type was set in Goshen.
The illustrations were created with mixed media: watercolor, gouache, acrylic, and digital.

Mum Bett fought for freedom during the American Revolution. Ida B. Wells would not be stopped. Rosa Parks and Claudette Colvin would not be moved. They took up space—because we all have the right to take up a little space in this world.

Prathia Hall preached in a way that made even Dr. King stop and listen. Lelia Foley became America's first Black female mayor because she knew that Black women could (and should!) lead cities. Because of her, we know that we can lead countries, too.

Phillis Wheatley wrote poetry so well that she challenged the thinking of an American president. And she paved the way for Mari Copeny, who demanded that a president give clean water to the residents of Flint, Michigan. Mari believed that a president should listen to her because all those women who came before her showed her that her voice matters, too.

With this book, I want to reach the little girls like me before society convinces them that their color and gender determine what they can dream and be. The women and girls in this book inspire us to speak up, command the space that is ours to take, fight for what we believe, make the world better for others, and always, always dream!

I want to pass on what Rosa gave me. I want to teach little girls to shine.

—BRITTNEY COOPER